LITTLE HAMSTER

BY LUCY KINCAID

ILLUSTRATED BY PAMELA STOREY

BRIMAX BOOKS · NEWMARKET · ENGLAND

Little Hamster is in his garden. He is busy. He is digging.
Red Fox stops at the gate.
Red Fox gives Little Hamster a letter.
"Who is it from?" says Little Hamster.

"Open it and see," says Red Fox. Little Hamster opens the letter.

"It is from Big Hamster," he says,

"He is coming to stay with me."

"When is he coming?" says Red Fox.

"He is coming on Monday," says Little Hamster.

Little Hamster meets his friends.

"Big Hamster is coming to stay," says Little Hamster.

"When is he coming?" says Bob Hedgehog.

"He is coming on Monday," says Little Hamster.

"How is he coming?" says Polly Pig.

"He is coming by train," says Little Hamster.

Little Hamster waits for Big Hamster. His friends wait with him. Along comes the train. It stops. Big Hamster gets off the train.

"Hallo!" says Big Hamster.

"Hallo, Big Hamster," says Little Hamster.

"I will take the bag," says Bob Hedgehog.

They go to Little Hamster's house. Big Hamster unpacks his bag. He has a straw hat. He puts it on. He has a stick. He picks it up. Little Hamster sits on the bed. His friends sit on the bed. Big Hamster sings a song.

"Big Hamster sings on the stage," says Little Hamster.

Big Hamster can dance. He does a tap dance. His feet go tap, tap, tap.
Big Hamster likes to dance. They all like to see Big Hamster dance.

Big Hamster is on the train.
Big Hamster is going home.
"Goodbye," says Big Hamster,
"Goodbye," says Little Hamster.
"Goodbye," says Bob Hedgehog.
"Goodbye," says Polly Pig.
"Goodbye," says Cheepy Chick.
The train puffs away. Big Hamster has gone.

The friends go home. They sit in the garden.

"I wish Big Hamster was here," says Little Hamster.

"So do I," says Bob Hedgehog.

"So do I," says Polly Pig.

"So do I," says Cheepy Chick.

They all look sad. They all feel sad.

Little Hamster gets up.

Little Hamster puts on a hat. He picks up a stick. "I will sing to you," he says.
"I will sing like Big Hamster." Little Hamster sings. He rolls his hat. He throws his stick. His friends clap. They still look sad. They still feel sad. They still wish Big Hamster was there.

Little Hamster wants his friends to smile. He gets on the table.

"What are you doing?" says Cheepy Chick.

"I am going to dance," says Little Hamster. "I am going to dance like Big Hamster."

Little Hamster tries to dance. He drops his stick. He drops his hat. His feet get mixed up. He looks very funny.

They all laugh.
"You are funny," says Bob
Hedgehog.
"You are funny," says
Polly Pig.
"You are funny," says
Cheepy Chick.
Little Hamster is so funny.
They think he is so funny.
They fall over.
Little Hamster is happy. His
friends are happy again.

"Watch me," says Little Hamster. He stands on one leg. He turns round.
"Oh!" says Little Hamster. "I am falling!"
Polly Pig catches him. He is not hurt.
"It is fun to dance," says Little Hamster. "Come and dance with me."

They all find a hat. They all find a stick. They all dance. They dance on the grass. It is safe on the grass. They will not be hurt if they fall.

"I wish Big Hamster could see us," says Little Hamster.

"So do I," says Bob Hedgehog.

"So do I," says Polly Pig.

"So do I," says Cheepy Chick.

Say these words again

garden	train
digging	catches
Monday	funny
friends	smile
unpacks	laugh
dance	goodbye
throws	mixed